LEVEL 2 READER

The Magic School Bus Rides Again

Rock Man vs. Weather Man

by Samantha Brooke

Scholastic Inc.

Arnold

Dorothy Ann (D.A.)

Wanda

Carlos

Keesha

Ralphie

Jyoti

Tim

ISBN 978-1-338-25378-8

10 9 8 7 6 5 4 3 2 1   18 19 20 21 22
Printed in the U.S.A.   40

First printing 2018
Book design by Jessica Meltzer

Meet Ms. Fiona Frizzle! No other science teacher is quite like her. She takes her class on wild science field trips. Her Magic School Bus twirls and whirls and can go anywhere.

Where will the bus take them today?

Ms. Frizzle's class is making a
time capsule, and everyone will put
something special inside of it.

Then they will bury it in the earth.
In the future, a new class will dig up
the time capsule and find the cool
things inside.

Keesha is putting in bracelets
and D.A. is adding research charts.

Tim wants to make a comic,
but he doesn't know what story
to draw.

"I'm putting in a Weather Man comic," says Ralphie.

"I'm putting in a Rock Man poster," says Arnold.

The boys argue about which superhero is stronger.

"I've got it!" says Tim. "I'll draw their battle for my comic."

Later, Tim asks, "How should I start my story?"

Suddenly, Ms. Frizzle leaps into the classroom dressed like a superhero.

"Start with some action. To the bus!" she cries.

The bus twirls and whirls. It transforms into a helicopter and zooms away.

"Welcome to Iceland, where we can see the real-life battle between rock and weather!" says Ms. Frizzle.

"And I can get ideas for my superhero comic," says Tim.

"This mountain is made out of **igneous rock**," says Arnold. "Nothing can destroy it."

"I bet the power of weather can," says Ralphie.

"Not a chance!" snaps Arnold.

The two boys argue if rock or weather is stronger.

"Now I know how to start the story," says Tim.

He draws a character who says, "I am Igneous Rock Man and nothing can destroy me!" The rocky superhero is wearing glasses just like Arnold's.

Tim draws another character who says, "I'm Weather Man, and I'm going to knock you down!"

This superhero has a hat like Ralphie's.

Weather Man shoots wind and lightning at Igneous Rock Man, but he doesn't break apart.

"I knew you couldn't defeat me," laughs the rocky hero.

Tim draws a new character who looks like Carlos.

"I bet I can defeat you with the help of Water Boy," says Weather Man.

"He's no match for me!" shouts Igneous Rock Man.

Water Boy and Weather Man blast the rocky hero with all their power.

They make cracks in the rock.

Tim takes a break from telling the story.

"This battle can last for centuries," says Ms. Frizzle.

"But that's hundreds of years!" cries Ralphie.

"This is when the battle gets cool," says Ms. Frizzle.

"Cool like ice?" asks Tim. "That's a fun story idea."

Tim goes back to telling the story.
Every winter, Water Boy fills the cracks in
Igneous Rock Man with water. When the
water freezes into ice, it **expands** and pushes
open the cracks.

Finally, pieces of the rocky hero break off and he **disintegrates**.

The broken pieces of rock fall into the river.

"Looks like weather beats rock!" shouts Weather Man.

"The end!" Tim says.

"Not so fast," says Ms. Frizzle. "The battle isn't over yet."

"Maybe something happens to the disintegrated rock bits?" Arnold asks.

"Smashing idea!" says Ms. Frizzle. Then she presses a button on the bus.

POOF! The kids turn into rocks and tumble down the mountain.

"This is one bumpy ride!" says Carlos.

Finally, the kids splash into the river, but their adventure isn't over yet.

"I'm going to be sick," groans Arnold.

As the rocks rush downstream, they **erode** into smaller and smaller pieces.

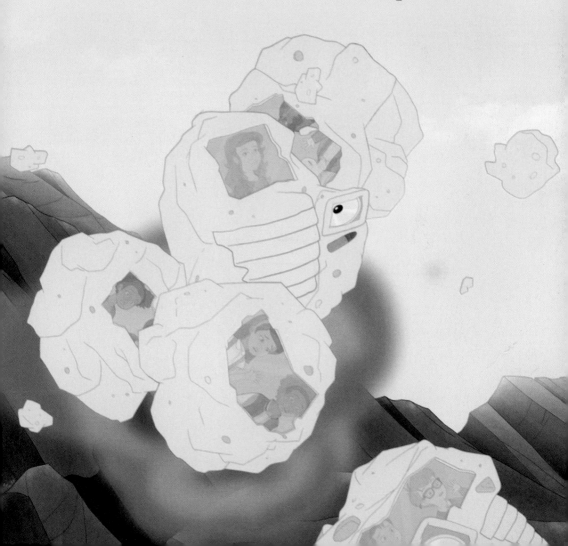

Finally, the kids wash up on the shore and turn back to normal.

"Class, you were turned into **clast**," says Ms. Frizzle.

"According to my research, clast is eroded bits of rock found in the river," says D.A.

"So what now?" asks Carlos.

Tim goes back to writing his comic.
In the next part of the story, Water Boy
returns to help Igneous Rock Man.
"I'm sorry for eroding you into clast.
Maybe I can stick you back together?"
he asks.

Water Boy needs a special kind of glue to do this. He makes that glue from materials in the earth.

Slowly, layer by layer, Water Boy glues the rocky hero's clast together.

"Ha! Now I'm back as **Sedimentary Rock** Man," he cheers.

"This cannot be happening!" cries Weather Man.

"I win!" shouts the rocky hero.

D.A. interrupts Tim's story.

"The battle can't be over! The girls aren't in the story," she says.

"I'm feeling a lot of heat and **pressure**," says Tim.

"Exactly right, Tim!" says Ms. Frizzle. "Heat and pressure come next!"

Over time, Sedimentary Rock Man gets pushed deep in the earth. So Tim draws three new characters that look like D.A., Wanda, and Keesha.

One uses fire to heat the rocky hero. The others use pressure to squeeze him.

The battle goes on for a million years. Could this be the end?

After a very long time, the rocky
hero rises up from the earth.
Now he is transformed into
Metamorphic Rock Man.
"You can change me, but you can't
defeat me!" he cries.

"Rock Man can't win!" yells Ralphie.

"Yeah! And the story can't be over until I'm in it," says Jyoti.

"I'm going to explode!" cries Tim.

"Okay, one explosion coming up," says Ms. Frizzle.

Ms. Frizzle hits the VOLCANO button. The bus twirls and whirls and lands inside a volcano.

"Look at all that hot **magma**! Magma is melted rock," says Ms. Frizzle.

"That gives me a hot idea," says Tim.

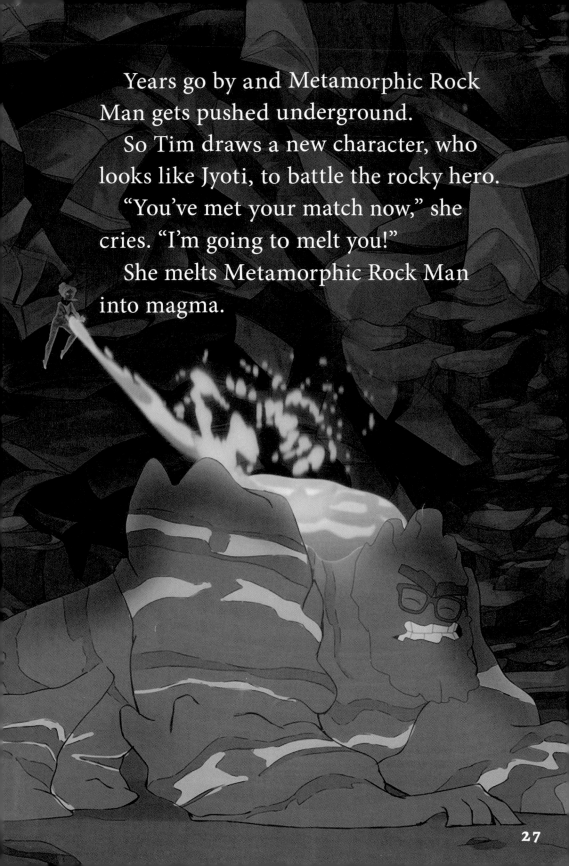

Years go by and Metamorphic Rock Man gets pushed underground.

So Tim draws a new character, who looks like Jyoti, to battle the rocky hero.

"You've met your match now," she cries. "I'm going to melt you!"

She melts Metamorphic Rock Man into magma.

Then something rises up from a crack in the earth.

"I'm back! And now you can call me Magma Man!" he says. "As soon as I cool off, I'll become a new kind of rock."

"Now that I'm cool, you can call me Igneous Rock Man," he says. "I'm the same kind of rock I began as."

"Nooooo!" shouts Weather Man.

The final victory goes to Rock Man!

Tim holds up his finished comic.
"Wahooo!" shout the kids.
"You can change Rock Man, but you can't beat him," says Arnold.
"That's the rock cycle," says Ms. Frizzle. "Igneous to Sedimentary to Metamorphic and back to Igneous. In the end, you go back to the beginning."

The Magic School Bus takes the kids back to school.

Tim puts his comic in the time capsule.

"Every rock has a story. It's never ending," says Tim.

"I told you rocks are unbeatable!" says Arnold.

Professor Frizzle's Glossary

Hi, I'm Ms. Frizzle's sister, Professor Frizzle. I used to teach at Walkerville Elementary. Now I do scientific research with my sidekick, Goldie. I'm always on an adventure learning new things, so here are some words for you to learn, too! Wahooo!

clast: A piece of rock that came from the breakdown of larger rocks

disintegrate: To break up into small parts

erode: To wear away slowly

expand: To become larger

igneous rock: A kind of rock or mineral formed by the cooling of magma

magma: Hot liquid found below the earth's surface

metamorphic rock: A kind of rock formed deep within the earth when heat or pressure is applied to igneous or sedimentary rocks

pressure: The action of pressing or pushing against something

sedimentary rock: A kind of rock formed by layers of sand, mud, and pebbles